My Shoes take me Where I Want to Go

by Marianne Richmond

My Shoes take me Where I want to Go

LCCN 2005907882

Marianne Richmond Studios, Inc.
420 N. 5th Street, Suite 840
Minneapolis, MN 55401
www.mariannerichmond.com

ISBN 0-977465160

Illustrations by Marianne Richmond

Book design by Sara Dare Biscan

Printed in USA

First Printing

My Shoes take me Where I want to Go

is dedicated to
my kids. — MR

When I
was born,
my mom
tells me,
I came
without
my clothes.

bare!

bare!

bare!

I can't imagine, I tell her,

having feet just bare,

Basketball Schedule

'cause now I have all kinds of shoes

that take me everywhere!

15

sneakers →

way to go! yeah!! woo-hoo!

My **sneakers** take me to the court
where I'm the fastest pro.

My team's behind when I **SLAM DUNK**
to cheers of

"way to go!"

My shoes that come with **bottom bumps** make me a **soccer star.** The tired goalie cannot rest...

bottom bumps

I **score** from **near** and **far!**

My **ice skates** bring me center rink
in hockey's biggest game.

My slap shot **wins**
in overtime.

Fans **jump** and **SHOUT**

_my_ name!

On rainy days, my red **galoshes**

take me out to sea.

I'm a **pirate** seeking buried treasure

in lands **so far** from me.

treasure

My **sandals** take me to the beach
with waves and water grand.

with **COWBOY BOOTS** and big ol' hat,
I'm **famous** in the **WEST**

It's my **hiking boots** that lead me up **high** mountains in the air.

My **leather mocs** with fluffy fur
make me an ESKIMO.

I fish through ice for family supper
and play all day in snow!

My **Sunday shoes** and cleanest pants

My Shoes

take me where I want to go

from where I am today.

They let me be the **different** things

that **I can be** <u>some</u> day.

But when I do get tired (yawn) from all I do and see,

my **slippers** take me to mom's lap,

where I'm *just* her *little* **me!**

slippers
quack quack

A gifted author and illustrator, Marianne Richmond
lives in Minneapolis, Minnesota with her husband, Jim,
and their four children.

The idea for "Shoes" came about years ago as Marianne
listened to Jim help their toddler son put on his shoes
to go outside. *"Your shoes take you where you want
to go,"* Jim said, *"inside, outside and to the park."*
Marianne sat down that day and wrote most of this
book. It just took awhile to do the pictures!

Marianne continues to create products that help people
connect with those who mean the most to them. Her
repertoire includes books, stationery and giftware.

Marianne shares her unique spirit and enchanting
artwork in her other titles: **The Gift of an Angel, The
Gift of a Memory, Hooray for You!, The Gifts of Being
Grand, I Love You So..., Dear Daughter,** and **Dear Son.**
Plus, she now offers the **Simply Said...** and
Smartly Said... mini book titles for all occasions.

www.mariannerichmond.com.